Aliens in the Basement

Suzan Reid

Illustrations by
Susan Gardos

Scholastic Canada Ltd.

For Ashley, Kaitlin and Maegan; June and Nelson Miles
(Mom and Dad) — thanks for checking my work!;

the students at Peachland Elementary;

and Nicol and Devyn — thanks for the daily inspiration.

Canadian Cataloguing in Publication Data

Reid, Suzan, 1963–

　　Aliens in the basement

(Shooting star)

ISBN 0-590-12392-0

I. Title.　II. Series.

PS8585.E607A84 1997　　　jC813'.54　　　C97-930535-7

PZ7.R44 A1 1997

4 3 2 1

Printed in Canada

7 8 9/9

Contents

Chapter 1

The Mess

"Matt Dias, run and get Mr. Turkle," said Mrs. Rupert, "and we'll get this mess cleaned up."

Matt froze. Everyone stopped planting marigolds and looked at him. Mrs. Rupert was struggling with a large bag of dirt, which was spilling out onto the floor.

"There must be a hole in the bag," said Mrs.

Rupert. "Quickly, Matt, before someone steps in this and tracks dirt all over the school. Find Mr. Turkle, and ask him for the big broom."

Matt started to feel queasy. "Can someone come with me?"

"It only takes one person to find Mr. Turkle. Please, Matt, before we have a mountain in our classroom!" Mrs. Rupert was now standing in dirt up to her ankles.

"Okay, okay, I'm going," Matt said as he made his way to the door.

"Don't worry," whispered Jaime Forrester as Matt brushed by her desk, "I'm right behind you."

Fulton Street School was an old school. It had been built in 1914, and the original building had only had four classrooms. Matt's classroom this year was in the newer section of the school. It was next to the gym, with the water fountain right outside the door. It was also close to the playground, so Matt's class was always first on the swings and tires at recess. But the old part of the school wasn't close to anything. The old part of the school gave Matt the creeps.

The janitor's room was in the basement of the old part of the school. Matt had never been down there. No one in his right mind would want to — everyone was afraid of Mr. Turkle. Mr. Turkle had been the janitor for a long time. He was a very tall man with a bushy face. He looked grumpy all the time.

Just the other day all the kids were talking about him at recess.

Thomas Webber said, "You know what I've heard? A long time ago, a kid went down to the basement and lost his memory or something."

Then Jaime added, "I've heard Mr. Turkle has a fridge down there that's full of all the good things that go missing out of everyone's lunches."

Matt's stomach grumbled whenever he remembered the day a double-chocolate brownie disappeared from his lunchbag.

Then Matt's big sister Zoe came by.

"That's nothing," she said. "You know what I've heard? There's a dungeon behind Mr.

Turkle's office, and all the bad kids have to go down there after school. Mr. Turkle is the only one who has the key and he makes you say your times tables over and over again before he lets you out."

Then she turned and left. All the kids just shook their heads in disbelief.

"I don't believe any of that stuff," thought Matt as he made his way toward the door at the end of the hall. "I'm just going to get a broom and take it back to class."

Finally, he reached the door. Taking a deep breath, he pulled it open — just a crack. It creaked and groaned. Matt peered down the stairwell. There was a light on at the bottom.

"Hello?" he called softly. There was no answer. Matt opened the door wider and reached for the railing. He took two steps down. "Hello?" he called again.

"Hey you!" came a loud voice. Matt jumped.

Chapter 2

Down the Dark Staircase

Matt looked over his shoulder slowly . . . and breathed a sigh of relief. "Jaime."

"I told you I'd be right behind you." Jaime grinned. "Did you really think I'd let you come down here all by yourself? I want to see what's down here."

"Where are you supposed to be?"

"Girls' washroom." Jaime brushed her brown bangs away from her forehead and leaned

against the doorway. "So I've only got a couple of minutes."

Matt and Jaime had been friends since they were babies. Their moms had worked together at the hospital, and they had taken turns babysitting when Matt and Jaime were little. Matt considered Jaime his best friend, even if people teased him about always hanging around a girl.

Jaime was always trying to find a way to get out of class — especially when it involved something exciting, like going down to the basement of the school. She loved adventure. Matt's mom said she loved it so much, she had a way of making up her own.

Matt waved a finger at Jaime. "You know, I almost wiped out on these stairs. Why did you have to yell like that? You're always making me jump."

"Oh, you're just jumpy, Matt! Now, come on," said Jaime, "let's go find Mr. Turkle."

Matt's hand skidded along the railing as he tiptoed down the dark staircase.

"Hurry up," said Jaime. "I'm going to trip right over you."

"Well, stop pushing me, then."

"I'm not pushing you. I'm guiding you in the right direction."

When they reached the basement, Matt called out again, "Hello?"

"Why are you whispering?" asked Jaime.

"I'm not whispering," whispered Matt.

"Sorry, I thought you were," Jaime whispered. They blinked to adjust to the dim light. Boxes were stacked in rows up to the ceiling along one wall, and old desks lined another. Matt glanced up and saw long strands of cobwebs. "It's creepy down here," he said.

"Smells funny, too." Jaime sniffed the stale air. "Like an old closet or something."

"Come on," Matt said, turning toward the stairs. "I don't think Mr. Turkle is down here. Let's go back —"

"Hey, look at this!" Jaime cried, lifting the lid off one of the boxes. Dust flew everywhere. Jaime waved it away. "Look at all these glass jars." She pulled one out and used her sleeve to wipe away the grime.

"What's inside?" asked Matt.

Jaime peered closely at it. "Nothing. It's empty," she said, "and I can't read the label."

"You're not wearing your glasses, that's why," Matt said. He looked around anxiously. "We should get out of here."

"Forget the glasses. Who needs them?" Jaime handed the jar to Matt and pulled out another. Matt grabbed them both from her and closed them up in the box. "Let's go." He looked up to see Jaime taking the lid off another box.

"These jars are bigger," she said, straining to lift one out, "and they have stuff in them."

"Probably pickles. Come on, Jaime, I mean it, let's go."

"No, check it out. There's some kind of liquid in this one." She rubbed at the label. "I still can't read it. Here, you take this one. Do you think these belong to Mr. Turkle?"

"Why would they belong to Mr. Turkle?" asked Matt, struggling with the big, slippery jar.

"Shh!" Jaime waved a hand in the air. "Listen! Do you hear something?"

They listened.

Someone was talking. It was hard to make out, but someone was definitely talking.

"Who is it?" asked Matt.

"I'm not sure," Jaime whispered.

"Mr. Turkle?"

"It doesn't sound like him." Jaime strained to hear.

"I can't understand the words," whispered Matt.

"Me neither. It's a weird-sounding voice." Jaime peered down the dark corridor. "That must be the door to Mr. Turkle's room."

Matt's eyes opened wide. The dungeon, Matt thought. Someone is in the dungeon.

"Matt!" Jaime yelled. "The jar!"

Too late. Matt fumbled and Jaime dove for it, but the jar went crashing to the cement floor. Jaime collided with Matt, and the two of them landed in a heap.

All of a sudden, a door flew open. "Who's down here?" It was an angry, rumbling voice.

Chapter 3

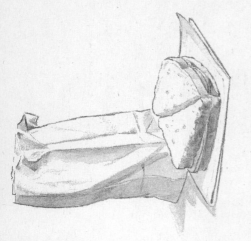

Something Secret

"Mr. Turkle!" Matt yelped as he and Jaime scrambled to their feet.

"Who's down here?" Mr. Turkle bellowed again.

Matt and Jaime shrieked.

"We . . . we . . ." started Matt.

" . . . need a broom!" sputtered Jaime. Then they both raced up the stairs without another

word, and without the broom.

They sped through the hallway toward their classroom.

"Whoa, cowpokes, where's the fire?"

Matt and Jaime skidded to a halt to avoid running into Mr. Douglas, the school principal. Matt tried to speak. "We were . . . we were . . . "

" . . . looking for a broom," Jaime blurted.

"I see." Mr. Douglas smiled. "And did we find one?"

"No . . . Yes! I mean, no," panted Matt.

"We asked Mr. Turkle," said Jaime.

"Mm hmm. Down in the basement, were we?"

"Yes. No. I mean — " started Matt.

"We *forgot* the broom," interrupted Jaime.

"Whoops!" She smacked her forehead. Matt glared at her.

"Well, you know," said Mr. Douglas, "that kind of running could cause an accident. We wouldn't want an accident, would we?"

"No, sir. We'll slow down," said Matt.

"Good news!" Mr. Douglas said with a smile.

"Ah! Here comes Mr. Turkle."

Matt and Jaime turned to see the janitor thundering down the hall toward them.

"Can we go now, please?" asked Jaime.

"Of course. Saunter along, now. No galloping."

Mrs. Rupert raised an eyebrow at Matt and Jaime when they burst into the classroom. She was teaching a lesson at the blackboard. The floor around her desk was covered in brown dirt.

"My goodness, that took you an awfully long time, Matt," Mrs. Rupert remarked drily. "And where were you, Jaime?"

"Line-up in the girl's washroom?"

"Uh huh." Mrs. Rupert frowned. "Matt? Where's the broom?"

Matt swallowed hard. Mrs. Rupert stared. Then there was a thump at the door.

"Oh, good. Here's Mr. Turkle now. Hello!" Mrs. Rupert smiled. "We need a little clean-up in here."

Mr. Turkle stomped into the classroom with

the broom and started sweeping furiously.

Matt slid down in his chair, opened up his math textbook and peered over it.

"He looks grouchy," whispered Jaime, from her desk one row up.

"He looks more than grouchy. He looks mad," whispered Matt.

"Well, we're saved for now," said Jaime.

"For now," Matt said as he slid back behind his math book.

* * *

Matt took his usual seat in the noisy lunchroom and saved the place next to him for Jaime. They had been sitting in the same lunchroom seats since grade one. The big kids usually sat at the back of the room — they were really loud and got into trouble all the time. The little kids sat right in front of the counter. Matt and Jaime sat at a table in the middle.

"Hey, Matt." Jaime plunked herself down and lifted the lid from her lunch tray. "You should get on the hot lunch program. Check out this spaghetti. Yum, yum," she said, waving her plate under his nose. "What have you got?"

"Meat and mustard. Want to trade?"

"Doubtful!" said Jaime, wrinkling her nose. "What else do you have?"

"Let's see . . . " said Matt as he rummaged through his bag. "Cookies?"

"The ones your mom makes?" asked Jaime. "Homemade. Smell." Matt unwrapped the cookies and waved them under Jaime's nose.

"Yum yum."

"Okay. I'll give you some of my spaghetti if you give me a couple of your cookies."

"Deal."

"So," said Jaime, as she chewed on a cookie, "what do you think?"

"I don't know. What do you think?" asked Matt.

"I think there's something strange down in the basement. I mean, what about that voice? What kind of language was that?"

"I don't know." Matt shrugged and sent his sandwich wrapper sailing over Jaime's head into the garbage can. Two points! "I don't know if I want to know."

"Look, Matt. Mr. Turkle was pretty upset that we were there. If you ask me," she said, as she passed him some spaghetti, "there's a secret downstairs."

"What kind of secret?" asked Matt.

"An it's-spooky-and-there's-something-weird-going-on kind of secret," answered Jaime.

"You're imagining things again," said Matt as he twirled his spaghetti. "It's probably nothing."

Jaime gave Matt a sharp look. "Have I ever been wrong before?"

"Yeah, lots of times."

"Well, this time I'm right. I think there's something going on down there, and I'm going back to take a closer look. Are you coming with me?"

Matt looked at the ceiling and sighed. "Well, someone's got to keep you out of trouble, so I guess I'd better."

Jaime grinned. "That's the spirit. Now, how

do we get down there without getting caught? Mr. Douglas always seems to show up when we're getting into something."

They spent the rest of the lunch hour discussing a plan.

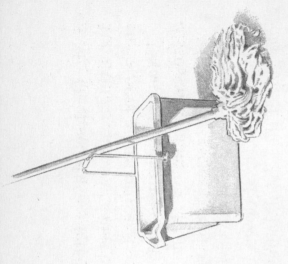

Chapter 4

The Toilet Trick

The bell rang at three, as usual. Matt and Jaime, however, did not do what they usually did. They usually went to get a basketball to shoot hoops for half an hour before riding home on their bikes.

Instead, they went to the library.

"Where is he?" asked Matt, peering through the window at the parking lot.

"There. There he goes." said Jaime.

Mr. Douglas always left right at five past three on Tuesdays because he had meetings at the School Board office.

"Wait until he drives away," said Matt.

"Okay, he's gone," Jaime whispered. They watched the black car pull out of the driveway and disappear down the street.

Then they tiptoed down the hallway to the old part of the school. Jaime opened the stairwell door, then paused.

"I can hear that voice again," she whispered. "Listen."

Matt and Jaime poked their heads through the doorway.

The strange voice rose faintly up the stairs. It was not Mr. Turkle's voice. At least, it didn't sound like Mr. Turkle's voice.

"Who is it?" whispered Matt.

"What is it?" said Jaime. "I don't understand anything."

"Okay, Jaime," urged Matt, "hurry up. You know what to do."

"It looks kind of dark down there."

"You don't have to go all the way down."

"I know." Jaime brushed her bangs off her face and began edging her way down the creaky stairs.

"Mr. Turkle?" she called. They waited.

"I don't think he heard you. Call him again," said Matt.

"Mr. Turkle?"

"Louder!" said Matt.

"Mr. Turkle!" shouted Jaime. The strange voice stopped. The basement was silent. Then they heard a chair thudding across the floor and two heavy footsteps. Jaime glanced up toward Matt. "I think he heard me this time."

"Who's down here?" bellowed Mr. Turkle's voice from behind his closed door. "Who's down in the basement?"

"It's Jaime, Mr. Turkle."

"What do you want?" Mr. Turkle roared.

"Well, um, there's an emergency upstairs, and I think you'd better come." Jaime glanced up the stairs to make sure that Matt was still there.

"What kind of emergency?" demanded Mr. Turkle.

"I, um, think that one of the toilets is leaking because there's water all over the floor in the girls' washroom."

"Psst . . . what's he doing now?" Matt whispered.

"He's moving stuff around. I can hear lots of clanging," Jaime whispered back.

"Clanging?" asked Matt.

"Yeah. A 'clang-clang' kind of sound."

Suddenly, Mr. Turkle appeared at the bottom of the stairs, holding a mop and a bucket in one enormous hand. He yanked on his very long beard with his other hand and scowled at Jaime.

"Let's go, then," he said. "I don't have all day."

Matt scrambled around the corner just as Mr. Turkle burst through the stairwell door, muttering, "Kids plugged up the toilets again."

Matt could hear Jaime whispering, "Let's go! Come on!" He scrambled around the corner and disappeared down the stairway into the darkness.

Chapter 5

Out of This World

"W here's the light switch?" Matt asked.

"I don't know. Feel around for it." Jaime felt the wall beside her and let out a yelp.

"What?"

"I found a huge spider's web."

Matt sighed. "Spiders won't hurt you."

Jaime shivered. "Let's just find Mr. Turkle's room. I think it's down this way. Where are you?"

"I'm right in front of you." Matt waved his arms around in the darkness. "We should have brought a flashlight down here. I didn't think he'd turn out all the lights."

"Never mind. Come on, let's go this way." Jaime grabbed Matt by the sleeve and tugged.

"You're walking too fast," said Matt. "I don't know what direction you're going in."

Jaime waved her arm around and hit a box.

"Oops," she said. "Let's try over —"

"Shhh! . . . Listen!" Matt whispered.

Then Jaime could hear it too: footsteps, getting louder, then thundering across the floor above them.

"Mr. Turkle!" they howled, and scrambled to find a place to hide.

"Over here!" shouted Matt. He ducked into a doorway and pulled Jaime in with him.

Mr. Turkle bounded down the stairs, muttering, "Leaky toilet. Leaky toilet, indeed!" His mop and bucket banged against the stairs all the way down. Matt could feel his heartbeat in his throat. Jaime held her breath.

"Kids," Mr. Turkle finally mumbled. He strode past the doorway where Matt and Jaime were standing and slammed the door to his room.

Matt and Jaime stood as still as they could.

"Listen," Matt finally whispered. "That strange voice again." He strained to listen.

But Jaime had begun to explore the storage room they were in. "Matt, you've got to see this," she said.

"What is it?" said Matt.

"This, here . . . you've got to look at this."

"Jaime, I'm trying to listen."

"I mean, this is really —"

"What, for crying out loud?" Matt stood up and turned to face Jaime. His eyes widened. "I don't believe it," he gasped. "What are they?"

"I don't know, but they sure are ugly," she whispered.

The room they were standing in was full of glass jars. There were small jars on the shelves around the room and large ones on the floor in the middle. Some of them had things floating inside. Things with strange heads.

"I've never seen anything like them before. They look like some kind of alien. Look at the ears on this one!" Jaime stepped closer to one of the jars and peered through the glass. "Look, Matt. Look how long the ears are!"

"I don't like it down here," said Matt.

Jaime peered inside another glass jar. "This one has long ears too," she noticed.

"It's creepy down here, Jaime. We'd better get out while we can," Matt insisted.

"We came down here to find out what's going on, so just hold on, would you?" Jaime said out loud.

"Be quiet!" whispered Matt. "He'll hear you!" Jaime glanced at him sharply and went back to examining the jar. "Very interesting."

"Maybe it's some kind of rabbit," Matt suggested. He shifted from one foot to the other and watched the doorway. "If he catches us . . ."

Jaime frowned at him. "Have you ever seen a rabbit with claws like this?"

"Claws?" asked Matt.

"Claws. Check it out."

Matt stepped closer to the large glass jar and peered inside. He jumped back in surprise. "I think it just waved at me."

They heard the strange, crackling voice again. Then they heard Mr. Turkle's voice.

Matt glanced back at the thing in the glass bottle. There it went again. "That thing *is* waving at me . . . " he whispered.

Jaime was too busy listening to the voices to hear him. "If I could only figure out what they're saying . . . " Then her eyes widened. "What if it's an alien language?" she gasped. She shook her hands in the air. "The things in these bottles could be little aliens!"

Matt felt a shiver run up his spine. "Let's get out of here."

They turned around slowly and crept out of the room. When they reached the stairs, they bolted for the top as fast as they could.

As they dashed down the empty hallway, they could hear a door opening with a bang, and Mr. Turkle bellowing, "Who's down here?"

"Keep running!" Jaime yelled.

"I plan to!" answered Matt, whizzing through the school doors behind her.

They unlocked their bikes, hopped on and didn't stop pedalling until they were ten blocks away.

Chapter 6

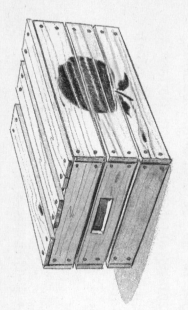

More Clues

They skidded to a stop at Matt's house. Leaving their bikes in a heap, they fled to the safety of Matt's secret treehouse. He pulled up the ladder and closed the door behind them.

"Do you think Mr. Turkle followed us?" Jaime gasped.

Matt shook his head. "I don't see anyone out there." He pulled up an old apple box to sit on.

Jaime's eyes were shining. "We have to get back down to the basement," she said.

"I was afraid you'd say that," Matt rolled his eyes.

"Oh, Matt. There's a real mystery right in front of you! We have to solve it!" Jaime's eyes widened. "If Mr. Turkle is listening to that alien language, then maybe *he's* an alien!"

Matt looked at her doubtfully.

"Or maybe he's been hypnotized," said Jaime, wagging a finger at Matt. "They took him onto an alien spaceship and taught him how to speak their language."

"But why?" asked Matt.

Jaime thought about it. "They're trying to take over the school!" she exclaimed.

"They're what?" asked Matt.

"They're taking over the school! They're growing aliens in the basement. Remember that show we saw on TV? The one that said there could be aliens on Earth? That's how they take over the world. They grow into people that look just like us."

"I remember," Matt nodded. "But why would they want to take over the school?"

"Maybe they want to learn something."

"Well, what can they learn that they don't already know?" Matt asked. "I thought aliens were supposed to be smarter than humans."

Jaime blew her bangs away from her eyes. "I don't know what they want to learn. Maybe they need to know our language. Like Zoe — she's learning French, right?"

Matt frowned. "Jaime, if what you're saying is true, then anybody in the school could be an alien."

"Maybe," said Jaime. She thought for a minute. "What about Eric Walters? He's pretty weird."

"That's true," Matt agreed. "He eats bits of glue and bites his nails. He also crosses his eyes whenever he looks at you."

"Right! And what about Cassie Jones?" asked Jaime. "Have you ever noticed that she seems to know the answer to everything? How does she do that? There's also Mr. Douglas. He has such a weird way of talking, and he's always sneaking up behind us. And Mrs. Rupert," said Jaime, "she could be one too."

"Mrs. Rupert?"

"Yeah," Jaime said, with a faraway look in her eyes. "She's always tapping her pencil on her desk. And when she's done tapping she sticks it above her right ear and lets it hang there. That's pretty weird."

"Maybe she's tapping out a secret code. Thomas Webber once told me that his dad taps out codes on his ham radio all the time."

"His *what* radio?" asked Jaime.

"Ham radio. His dad uses it to talk to people all over the world," answered Matt.

"And he uses a code?"

Matt shrugged. "Yeah. I forget what it's called. We could check it out with Thomas."

"Then we could figure out if Mrs. Rupert is tapping out secret messages," said Jaime. "Maybe there are other aliens in the classroom, and that's how they communicate with each other. I mean, they can't very well just talk in alien language, can they?"

They were quiet for a few minutes.

"Okay, so how would they get the aliens into the basement?" asked Matt.

"They would have to sneak them in. Probably late at night." Jaime stood up and stretched. "Well? Are we going to try to communicate with them? Or at least learn what their secret language is?"

"I don't know, Jaime," said Matt. "I don't know if I believe any of this. It all seems pretty weird."

"Hey twerp!" yelled a voice from down below. "Get out of your dollhouse and get supper going. Mom will be home soon."

"Speaking of aliens . . . " Matt said, nodding in Zoe's direction. "I'm coming!" he called back.

"Come on, Matt, I'm counting on you," said Jaime, as they climbed down from the tree-house. "What do you say?"

Matt scratched his head. "I'll think about it. I'll let you know tomorrow."

* * *

At the dinner table that night, Matt announced, "I'm not really that hungry."

"Nonsense," his mom replied. "You must be starving."

While Mrs. Dias loaded up Matt's plate with dinner, Zoe talked non-stop — about what her teacher did, what her teacher said, what her teacher didn't say, what the boys did, who the girls liked and who got into trouble.

Matt broke in. "Mom, do you think there are such things as aliens?"

Zoe's mouth dropped open and she turned to glare at him. "Excuse me, but I was right in the middle of talking."

"Matt, you shouldn't interrupt your sister," said Mrs. Dias.

"This is important," Matt said firmly.

"What was the question?" asked Mrs. Dias.

Matt pushed his peas around on his plate.

"Do you think there are aliens?"

Zoe let her fork fall on her plate and burst out laughing.

"Zoe, please . . . " Mrs. Dias turned to Matt.

"Well, Matt, I suppose that some people think they exist."

Zoe pulled on her face until her skin was tight and she had squinty eyes. "I'm an alien," she said in a funny voice.

"Zoe! Stop bothering your brother. Matt, just eat your dinner."

"Mom? Can I be excused? I really meant it. I'm not very hungry," said Matt.

Mrs. Dias reached across the table and felt Matt's forehead. "You're not hot. But go on up and finish your homework. I'll check on you later."

As he climbed the stairs to his bedroom, Matt looked out the landing window. A van drove slowly by. He could read the words on its side. "Rupert's Jar and Bottle Depot!" Matt gasped. He ran to his bedroom window to get a better look as it passed. He grabbed his binoculars. Sure enough, in the passenger's seat, there was Mrs. Rupert.

Chapter 7

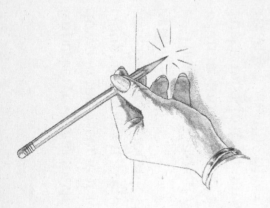

Trying to Communicate

The next morning, Jaime was in her usual spot at the end of the street.

"Hey, Jaime!" Matt pedalled up to meet her. He told her about the van.

Jaime's eyes widened in excitement. "What a perfect cover!" she exclaimed.

"Cover?"

Jaime was almost bursting. "Mr. Rupert picks up jars and gives them to Mrs. Rupert. Mrs.

Rupert gives them to Mr. Turkle. He keeps them down in the basement where nobody goes. Mr. Douglas keeps an eye on everyone and makes sure the secret doesn't get out. Oh, man, this is getting good!"

"Then what?" asked Matt.

Jaime thought for a moment. "Then Mr. Turkle talks to the aliens," she continued. "They arrange a meeting place. The aliens give him the things we saw in the bottles — the things that turn into people."

"It's incredible! This is actually starting to make sense," said Matt.

Jaime turned to face him and grinned. "Does this mean you're in?"

"I guess so," said Matt.

Jaime gave him a big high-five. "Great! I just *knew* you'd come through! Come on, we'd better get to school!"

Matt and Jaime took their seats while Mrs. Rupert entered with her usual pile of papers in one hand and a cup of coffee in the other. "Good morning," she said. "I hope you all remembered the math quiz. You have one minute to make sure you have a sharp pencil."

"Math quiz?" Jaime groaned.

Mrs. Rupert handed out the papers and the room went quiet. Matt wrote down his name and glanced around the room. Everything seemed normal. Mrs. Rupert was busy at her desk, looking through a textbook. Matt looked at the first question and started to write.

A few minutes later, Mrs. Rupert began tapping her pencil, very quietly, on the edge of her desk. Matt glanced up. He poked Jaime in the back with his pencil.

"I hear it too," Jaime whispered.

Matt leaned forward. "It's that code. Maybe she's trying to find out if there are other aliens in the classroom. Try tapping something back."

"Okay."

"Jaime?" Mrs. Rupert was looking right at her. "Is there a problem?"

"No," answered Jaime, "no problem."

After a minute, the tapping began again. *Tap . . . tap-tap-tap.*

Jaime answered, slowly and quietly. *Tap* . . . *tap-tap-tap*.

Matt stopped writing and waited.

Mrs. Rupert tapped again. *Tap* . . . *tap-tap* . . . *tap*.

Jaime took a deep breath and answered again. *Tap* . . . *tap-tap* . . . *tap*.

Mrs. Rupert started looking around the room. She tapped again.

This time Matt joined in. *Tap* . . . *tap-tap-tap*.

One by one, the other students in the classroom stopped writing and turned to look at Jaime and Matt.

Mrs. Rupert stood up. As she did, she tapped another message. *Tap* . . . *tap* . . . *tap* . . . *tap-tap*.

Matt and Jaime tapped the message back. Mrs. Rupert slowly tucked her pencil behind her right ear and walked out in front of her desk. Matt and Jaime put their pencils behind their right ears, too.

"What is going on here?" asked Mrs. Rupert as she approached Jaime's desk.

Jaime looked up at Mrs. Rupert. "Nothing," she replied.

"Why are you tapping your pencil?" Mrs. Rupert demanded.

"Was I tapping my pencil?" Jaime asked sheepishly.

"Yes, you were, and you know you were. You've disrupted the classroom, and now you're being defiant." She pointed toward the door. "Go and see what Mr. Douglas has to say. You too, Matt."

"I think she means it," Jaime whispered to Matt. In the hallway, she asked, "Do you think we communicated with her?"

"We communicated all right," sighed Matt as he plunked himself down on the bench outside Mr. Douglas's office, "just not the way we wanted to."

"I don't get it. She was definitely tapping some kind of code," said Jaime as she sat down.

"Yeah, it was a code, but how can we communicate if we don't know what the tapping means?" asked Matt.

Mr. Douglas stepped out of his office and motioned for them to come in.

"Well, cowpokes, you must have rustled up some trouble, or you wouldn't be here." Mr. Douglas sat down in his big chair and looked at them. "Which one of you is the leader of this gang?"

Matt looked at Jaime and raised an eyebrow. Jaime shrugged.

"Well." Mr. Douglas smiled. "It's the Jaime Forrester Gang, is it? Well, Jaime Forrester, I don't believe your gang has ever visited my office before."

"It's not a gang, Mr. Douglas — " Jaime began.

"Of course it's a gang." Mr. Douglas kept smiling as he pulled the lid off a container of jellybeans and poured a dozen into his hand. One by one, he popped them into his mouth. One, two, three, four. He was waiting for an answer.

"We were, uh, just tapping out, uh — oh yeah — just tapping our pencils while we were writing a quiz." Jaime finally answered.

Mr. Douglas looked interested. "Tapping your pencils? Why would you be doing that?"

Jaime wiggled in her chair. "Mrs. Rupert was tapping hers and we were trying to —"

Matt nudged her.

" . . . copy her," she finished.

"Anything else?" asked Mr. Douglas.

Jaime shook her head. "No, not really. She said I was being defiant."

Mr. Douglas popped the last jellybean into his mouth and stood up. "I see. Well, cowpokes, you owe Mrs. Rupert an apology. I guess she'll be keeping you after school. Now if I see you in my office again — either of you — you'll be on garbage detail. You know what that is, don't you?"

Matt and Jaime looked at each other and nodded. They had seen garbage detail. Kids had to take two big garbage bags and clean up all the litter around the fields and the back fence. It was not a nice job. But at least it wasn't the dungeon.

"I thought so. Well, saunter along, now."

"No galloping," Jaime added under her breath.

Matt and Jaime returned to the classroom just as Mrs. Rupert was collecting the math quizzes.

"I'll see you at three o'clock," she said. "You can write your tests then."

* * *

At three twenty-five, Matt glanced up from his test and peeked at the clock.

"You have five more minutes," said Mrs. Rupert from behind her desk. There was a knock on the door. Mrs. Rupert pushed back her chair and stood up. "Keep writing," she said as she opened the door. "Mr. Turkle! How are you today?"

Matt poked Jaime in the back with his pencil. "Are you almost finished?" he whispered.

"Almost," she whispered back. "I'll bet they're talking about the jars. Maybe they have a new load of aliens to bring into the basement."

"Or maybe they're talking about us," said Matt.

Jaime's eyes widened. "That's it, Matt, they must be. I think they're on to us."

Chapter 8

Radio Signals from Where?

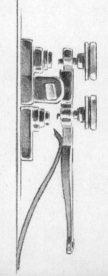

The next day was Saturday. Matt and Jaime got up early and biked over to Thomas's house.

"Come on in," Thomas yawned as he opened the door. "Dad's out back in the shed. I told him you were coming."

Thomas's dad had a ham radio shack in the far corner of the property. It had a huge tower with a bunch of wires attached to it, all going off in different directions.

"Can he really talk to people all over the world from that little building?" Matt asked Thomas.

"That's what he says." Thomas opened the door of the shack. "Hey, Dad."

Mr. Webber looked up from his operating equipment and waved. He finished saying something into a microphone, then took off his headphones. "Hey, you three. Nice to meet you, uh —"

"Jaime," she said, as she shook Mr. Webber's hand. "This is Matt."

"Nice to meet you, Jaime and Matt. I heard you wanted to know something about Morse code."

Jaime pulled up a chair beside Mr. Webber. "We were wondering if you could teach it to us," said Jaime.

Mr. Webber smiled. "Well, it's not that easy to learn," he said. "It takes a lot of time and practice. Here, I'll show you." Mr. Webber opened a filing cabinet and pulled out a large folder. "It's in here somewhere . . . Ah! Here we go!" He unfolded a large piece of paper. "Here's the alphabet."

Jaime stared at the dots and lines. "It sure looks like it could be some kind of alien language."

"Sure does, doesn't it?" said Mr. Webber.

Jaime glanced at Matt. "How does it work?" she asked.

"This is an A: dot, line." Mr. Webber tapped it out on his desk. "This is a B: line, dot, dot, dot."

"Why do people use Morse code? Couldn't they just talk to each other?" asked Matt.

"The sound of Morse code travels better than the human voice, especially over long distances," Mr. Webber explained.

Jaime glanced at Matt again. "So if you were trying to contact someone *really far away*, you would use Morse code."

"That's right," said Mr. Webber. "You can send messages over thousands of miles. It's also better to use Morse code when weather conditions are bad. It comes in a lot clearer than the human voice."

Matt examined the equipment on Mr. Webber's table. "There are lots of dials and knobs and stuff here."

"It's a great hobby," said Mr. Webber. As he spoke, a message began to come through the speaker. Mr. Webber turned in his chair and picked up a pencil and a pad of paper.

"What is it?" asked Jaime.

"Just a minute," said Mr. Webber.

"C.Q. . . . C.Q. . . . C.Q. . . . " said the crackling voice over the radio.

Mr. Webber put the headphones back on.

"C.Q.? What does that mean?" asked Jaime.

Thomas shrugged. "Beats me," he answered. "Dad's out here a lot. Sometimes he talks to people through the microphone, and sometimes he taps out Morse code on that thing over there, called a bug." He pointed to a small object on the desk.

Mr. Webber finished replying to the message and took off the headphones. "That one was from far away!" he exclaimed. "Now I'll see if I can find some Morse code." He turned a dial until they heard a faint tapping sound. "Not bad. But let's see if I can find a better one."

"Can you get messages from people from other galaxies?" asked Jaime. Matt nudged her.

"I mean, *could* you if there *were* people from other galaxies?" she added.

"This one sounds like it could be from another galaxy!" exclaimed Mr. Webber as a voice came through the speaker. He put the headphones back on and began scribbling notes on his pad of paper.

"Is he joking?" Matt asked Thomas.

Thomas shrugged. "I don't know."

Mr. Webber was on the microphone for a long time. While they waited for him to finish, Jaime and Matt examined the Morse code alphabet.

"We'll never learn this fast enough," said Matt.

"I guess you're right," Jaime nodded sadly.

Finally, Mr. Webber removed the headphones and smiled. "That was from Hong Kong," he said. He pulled a pin with a red flag on it from his desk drawer. He spun his chair

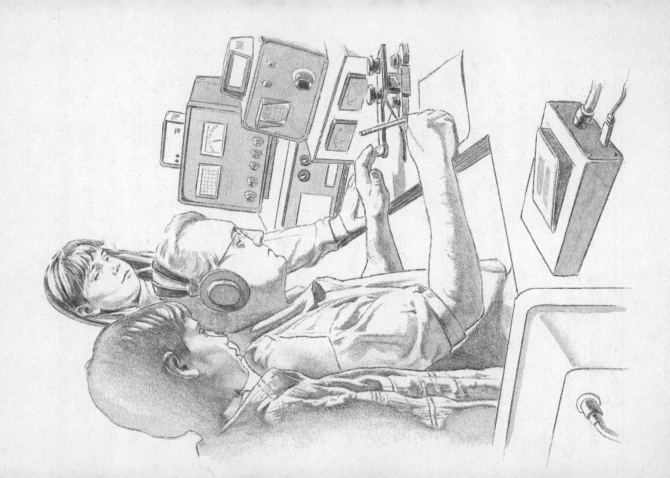

around and stuck the pin to a large map of the world. "Now, what else did you want to know about —" he stopped abruptly, and turned up the volume to hear a series of taps. "Excuse me again, I have to answer this one." He started tapping out a message on the bug.

"He's pretty good at that," Jaime said to Thomas. "Now, how about pencils? Does he ever tap pencils?"

"Pencils? What are you talking —"

"Listen, Thomas," Matt cut in, "your dad looks pretty busy. We should be going now." He reached for the doorknob. "Thank him for us, okay?"

Thomas nodded. "Sure, okay," he answered. Jaime and Matt headed for their bikes. "Did you *hear* Mr. Webber? Wow! Other galaxies!" said Jaime.

"Are you saying you think he's wrapped up in this somehow?"

"I'm saying we can't be too sure about anybody right now. Maybe there are more aliens out there than we know!" Jaime hopped on her bike. "Maybe the whole town is full of them! Maybe this has been going on for years!" She rode her bike in little circles around Matt. "I know! I know what we can do! On Monday, we can check the old newspapers in the library. We can find out if anything weird has happened before — you know, strange lights in the sky, or anything like that!"

"That's a great idea," agreed Matt.

"Matt . . . " Jaime stuck her foot out and stopped the bike. She suddenly looked worried. "Matt, how do I know that you're not an alien?"

Matt rolled his eyes. "Don't worry, Jaime, you would be the first to know. Now, let's get out of here," he said, getting on his bike. "I've got lots of errands to run for my mom."

Chapter 9

The Chase

They pedalled to a stop at a red light.

"Jaime, look who's over there," said Matt.

"Where?" Jaime asked, turning to look. There was a crowd of people crossing the intersection. "There. That guy walking really fast. Who does he look like?"

Jaime squinted. "I don't see anyone."

"You don't have your glasses on." Matt grabbed her by the shoulders and turned her to face the other direction. "Right there."

Jaime could make out a tall figure walking briskly along the sidewalk. "Is it . . . . "

"It's Mr. Turkle!" said Matt.

"I've never seen Mr. Turkle anywhere but at school," said Jaime. "It's weird to see him out in the sunshine. I wonder what he's doing here?"

"He's in a real hurry," said Matt. "What should we do?"

"We should follow him!" answered Jaime.

They waited anxiously for the light to change.

"Maybe he's going to meet another alien," said Jaime, "to find out when the next shipment of them is coming in!" The light finally turned green. "Come on!"

They walked their bikes across the intersection, then hopped on and sped to the next block. When they were half a block from Mr. Turkle they slowed right down.

"We can't let him see us," said Matt, as they rounded a corner.

"Look! He's going into the mall!" Jaime exclaimed.

Matt and Jaime parked their bikes, locked them up and followed Mr. Turkle into the Westside Mall. It was packed with people.

"It's a good thing he's tall," said Jaime as they darted in and out of the crowd, "or we'd lose him for sure."

"Wait!" Matt exclaimed. Mr. Turkle stopped at a newsstand and picked up a newspaper. Matt and Jaime slipped behind a large fake plant to watch him.

"Look what he's buying," whispered Jaime. Matt brushed the leaves away from his face.

"I've never seen Mr. Turkle read a newspaper before. Have you?" Jaime was leaning over Matt's shoulder. "Now he's flipping through the pages. What do you think he's looking for?"

"I can't see with your head in the way," said Matt.

"He's coming this way!" exclaimed Jaime.

"Quick! Hide!" Matt pulled Jaime over to the other side of the planter just in time to avoid being seen by Mr. Turkle, who was plunking himself down on the bench a few feet away from them. He flipped noisily through the newspaper, then finally seemed to find what he was looking for. He poked his big finger at the page as he read. Then he grinned. Matt and Jaime looked at each other, stunned.

"I've never seen him smile before," said Jaime. Then Mr. Turkle stood up and started walking away.

"He just threw the newspaper into that trash bin! Come on!" Matt and Jaime darted out from behind the plant and wove a path through the crowd until they reached the bin.

Jaime looked down into it. "Yuck. This is really disgusting," she said. "How about you fish it out and I'll keep an eye on Mr. Turkle?"

Matt rolled up his sleeve and reached deep into the bin. The paper had a banana peel stuck to it. Matt examined the page it was folded to. "This is a weather map. Big deal."

Jaime gasped. "Big deal? You can't very well land a spaceship in rotten weather, can you?" she said. "You'd have to know when the skies were going to be clear. Don't you see? They have to figure out where to land the spaceship!"

"Jaime, you're getting that funny look in your eyes again . . . "

"Look! He's going into that bookstore!" Jaime shouted.

Matt tossed the newspaper back into the bin and followed her into the store. It was cool and quiet in there. They crept silently between the rows of books until they saw Mr. Turkle. He was leafing through a fat paperback.

"What kind of book is that?" asked Jaime, poking her head between the cookbooks and gardening titles.

Matt glanced up at the sign hanging from the ceiling. "He's in the Travel section."

Jaime's eyes widened. "Maybe he has to go somewhere else, like a different city, or out in a desert somewhere, to meet the spaceship! I've heard of spaceships landing in the desert before."

Mr. Turkle took the book to the counter, spoke to the woman there for a moment, paid for the book and left.

"We can't lose him. Come on!" She dashed for the door, dragging Matt with her.

"Where did he go?" she asked as they peered through the crowd.

"Over there." Matt pointed. "He's going into the drugstore now."

Matt and Jaime ducked into the store behind Mr. Turkle. They followed him past long shelves of cough medicine, toothpaste and diapers.

Matt poked his head into aisle five and watched Mr. Turkle pull a funny pair of sunglasses off a rack and try them on.

"Those are pretty strange-looking glasses," he said.

"They're green! They look like alien eyes!" Jaime gasped. "It all makes sense! They're for protecting his eyes from the bright lights of the spaceship!"

Just then, Mr. Turkle looked over in their direction. They scrambled to hide around a corner. After a moment, they poked their heads back out.

"Where did he go?" asked Matt.

"He was right there!" said Jaime.

They began searching the aisles.

"How could we have lost him?" Matt cried.

"He was right —"

"Looking for someone?" a low voice rumbled.

Matt looked up.

"M-M-Matt . . ." Jaime stammered.

"Looking for someone?" the voice repeated. Matt looked way up. Staring down at him was a familiar face. It was bushy. It was frowning. It was Mr. Turkle.

Chapter 10

Back to the Basement

"Yes—no! I mean, yes . . . " Matt answered.

"We were just — " began Jaime.

"You've been following me around," said Mr. Turkle. His eyes were round and wide. "I saw you in the bookstore, and I saw you behind that plant." Mr. Turkle leaned down and stared into Matt's eyes. "Now why would you be following me around?"

"We — we — we —" Matt gulped.

Jaime lunged in front of Matt. "It was all my idea, Mr. Turkle! Please don't hurt him! We just want to go home!"

Mr. Turkle stood up and stepped back. He frowned. He scratched his forehead. "Crazy kids. Life must be pretty dull around here. Now look, kid. Don't worry," he said, rolling his eyes. "I'm not going to hurt you. But couldn't you just go shoot *hoops* or something? Sheesh." Then he brushed past them and went over to the cashier.

Jaime watched him go, biting her lip. Matt took a deep breath and let out a "Whew!"

As they walked back out into the mall, Jaime said, "He's on to us, all right. And he tried to throw us off his trail. Very tricky. But we know better." She stopped and turned to face Matt. "We have to get back down into Mr. Turkle's room. That's all there is to it. We have to get down to the bottom of this."

* * *

Monday morning, as Matt was finishing his breakfast, his mom walked into the kitchen.

"My goodness! What are you doing awake so early?" She was towel-drying her hair. "You're not due to get up for another half hour."

"I've got lots to do at school," Matt answered. He stacked his juice glass in the dishwasher.

Mrs. Dias smiled. "That's what I like to see! Doing a little extra research?"

"You could say that," Matt said as he grabbed his backpack and headed for the door. "I'll see you tonight."

The neighbourhood was quiet. Matt rode his bike down to the end of the street. There was Jaime, right where she always was.

"Have you got everything?" she asked as Matt approached.

"I've got the flashlight," he answered. They rode in silence. Finally, Jaime asked, "Are you scared?"

They pulled into the school parking lot. Matt shrugged. "I don't think so. Are you?"

Jaime shook her head. "Of course not!"

As they locked up their bikes, Matt spied something in the far corner of the parking lot. "The van!" he exclaimed. "That's the van that was driving down my street! Look, it says 'Rupert's Jar and Bottle Depot' on the side."

"They must be bringing in a new shipment," said Jaime. "Let's go check it out."

She ran ahead to the van, and Matt followed cautiously.

"I don't think there's anyone in it," Jaime said, "but the door is open a crack." She reached for the handle and pulled. It slid open. "Boxes! Just like the ones in the basement!" Jaime climbed into the van and opened one of the boxes. She pulled out a jar and showed it to Matt. They were exactly the same, all right.

"I wonder if they're taking them down to the basement or carrying them out," said Matt.

"There's only one way to find out," said Jaime. "Come on!"

They leaped up the steps and into the school.

"I've never seen it so empty in here," said Jaime. Matt covered her mouth. "There's an echo," he whispered.

Suddenly they heard voices.

"Quick! Into the office!" Matt hissed as he reached for the door. It wouldn't open. "It's locked!"

"Over here!" Jaime called. She shot across the hallway and held open a door. "Come on!" Matt followed her in. "See?" Jaime whispered, grinning. "The girls' washroom always comes in handy."

The voices outside were getting louder and louder. Matt pulled open the door just a crack.

"Who is it?" asked Jaime.

"It's Mrs. Rupert and someone else — I'd say Mr. Rupert," Matt whispered.

"What are they doing?"

"Shhh!" Mr. and Mrs. Rupert were just steps away. When they had passed, Matt let the door close. "They were carrying jars."

"Well, we'd better get down to the basement before they get back," said Jaime.

They darted out of the washroom and toward the basement stairs. Jaime pulled open the heavy door and switched on the light.

Matt reached over and switched it off. His flashlight clicked on. "We can't let anyone suspect we're here. Follow me." He led Jaime down the stairs and toward Mr. Turkle's room.

"What about the jars?" Jaime asked.

"We'll check those later. Come on. We're going to find out what's really in that room, and then we're getting out of here."

Just then, his flashlight started to flicker. "My battery's low." He knocked the flashlight a few times against the palm of his hand.

"Great." Jaime rolled her eyes.

The light got brighter. "There we go," said Matt. He waved the flashlight around until it shone on Mr. Turkle's door. It had big block letters on it that read "Janitor."

"This is it," Matt whispered. "The dungeon is supposed to be back here. Do you see any-thing?"

Jaime squinted through the darkness, then let out a terrible scream.

Chapter 11

A Voice in the Dark

"What is it?" Matt called. "What do you see?"

Jaime pointed down the dark corridor. "Over there."

Matt swung his flashlight around. "That? That spider?"

"I don't like spiders," Jaime answered. "And it's huge!"

Matt let out a sigh of relief. "I thought you'd found the dungeon. It's not huge. It's only a little guy."

"Well it looks huge to me." Jaime shivered.

"Come on, we don't have much time," Matt said. He pulled on the old wooden door, and it creaked open slowly.

The room was cluttered with pails, brooms and cleaning supplies.

"Look!" whispered Jaime. "I knew it! I knew there was a fridge down here!" She crossed the small room and opened the fridge door.

"What's inside?" asked Matt.

"Containers," Jaime answered.

"Containers of what?"

Jaime opened one of them. "This one has pickles in it."

"Pickles?"

Jaime opened another one. "This one's cheese." She checked them all. Bologna, lettuce, margarine. All of the containers had the name "Turkle" written on them.

Jaime sealed them and shut the fridge door.

"Nothing," she said disappointedly. "I thought there would be some great stuff in there."

As she moved away from the fridge, Matt's flashlight flickered again. It dimmed for a moment, then went out. They were left in total darkness.

"Matt? Matt?" Jaime's voice sounded panicky. "What happened, Matt? Where are you?" Matt knocked the flashlight against his palm again. *Thok, thok.*

Jaime shrieked. "Who's there? Matt, Matt, where are you?"

"I'm right here," Matt answered through the darkness. "Just relax, will you? I'm trying to get this thing to turn back on. Open the fridge again so we can have some light."

"Oh, what a relief! I thought you were — "
Jaime took a few steps toward the fridge and tripped over something on the floor. As she struggled to regain her balance, she knocked into something on a table. Then she noticed something odd. A small green light was glowing in front of her.

"Matt, look over here."

Matt was still trying to get the flashlight to work. "What?"

Jaime didn't get to answer, because suddenly, out of nowhere, a voice boomed through the darkness.

"Bwen-os dee-as," the voice said. "Good day."

Matt and Jaime screamed.

"It said my name! It said 'Dias'!" gasped Matt.

"Bwen-os dee-as," the voice repeated. "Good day."

Matt banged harder on the flashlight.

"Hurry, Matt, hurry!" urged Jaime.

Finally the flashlight flickered on. Matt waved it frantically around the room. "Who are you? Who's there?" he shouted. "Come on, we know you're here!"

Matt aimed the flashlight right at the green glow. Then he let out an enormous sigh. "It's . . . a tape recorder," he said.

"Bwen-os dee-as," the voice said a third time. "Good day."

"It's playing a tape," said Jaime.

"Ad-ee-os!" the voice continued. "Good-bye."

Matt pushed the eject button and pulled out the tape. "Simple Spanish," he read aloud.

He flashed his light around the rest of the workbench. A magazine was lying open in front of a big chair. Jaime grabbed it. "It's an article called 'Travelling Around Mexico,'" she said with a groan.

Matt collapsed into the chair. "Mr. Turkle must be going to Mexico for the holidays."

Jaime counted off on her fingers. "The newspaper — probably checking out the temperature in Mexico. The travel book — it's about Mexico. The funny sunglasses. It all makes sense!"

Matt rubbed his forehead. "I can't believe I actually let you talk me into this."

"Oh, come on, Matt. You believed everything, too. You're the one who discovered Rupert's Jars!"

"The jars!" Matt exclaimed. "We still don't

know what's in them!" He raced down the hall.

"Hurry up, Jaime!"

"I'm coming!" Jaime called as she stumbled through the dark behind him.

Matt shone the flashlight around the storage room. "Let's take one," he said. "We'll find out what these labels say in the library."

"Okay," agreed Jaime. "But you take it. I don't want to carry it."

Matt grabbed the jar with the long-eared, clawed creature in it, and headed up the stairs. They pulled open the door and looked down the hall. The coast was clear.

As they stepped into the library, the lights came on. "Someone's here!" whispered Jaime.

"No, no one's here. The lights are automatic, remember?" The library was in the newer part of the school.

Matt set the heavy jar on a table beside a computer terminal. "Let's hurry up," he said. "People will be coming to school soon."

Jaime glanced at the clock. "We have about fifteen minutes," she said.

"Okay, let's see what's in that jar." Matt spun the monitor around and clicked on the encyclopedia program.

Welcome to Smart Jr., said the message on the screen. *Please enter a keyword and I will perform a search for you.*

"Okay, now, what does the label say?" he asked.

Jaime turned the label of the jar toward her. She squinted to read the words. "I guess I should have brought my glasses," she said. Slowly she spelled out the words. "O-r-y-c-t-e-r-o-p-u-s a-f-e-r."

Matt keyed in the whole thing, then hit "Enter."

Nothing happened right away. Then the screen started to change colour.

Chapter 12

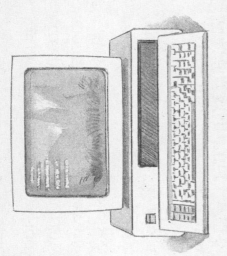

Everything Fits into Place

"There! Something's coming up. What is it?" asked Jaime.

Matt watched the image appearing on the screen. Then he put his head in his hands and moaned. "It's an aardvark," he said in a muffled voice.

"A what?" said Jaime, in disbelief.

"An aardvark. Take a look." They looked at

the picture of the strange-looking animal on the screen. It had a long narrow head and a long snout. It had rabbit-like ears and long claws.

"Well, you two cowpokes are certainly in early," said a voice from behind them. Matt and Jaime spun around. "Doing a little research, are we?"

"Yes, Mr. Douglas," answered Jaime. She looked at Matt. "But we're finished now."

Mr. Douglas walked up to the computer terminal. "Putting in a little extra effort before the holiday, hmm?" He smiled. "Well, that's mighty fine. I'm off to the ranch for the holiday, myself. Can't wait."

"Ranch?" asked Matt.

"My folks live on a ranch. Grew up there myself. I miss those horses and the cattle." He took a deep breath and smiled. "Nothing like the smell of a ranch."

"Well," said Matt with a sigh, "I guess we'll go outside until the bell rings." He started gathering up his things.

Mr. Douglas picked up the jar from the table.

"Are you finished with this?" he asked. "It's a fine African aardvark specimen, don't you think?"

Jaime gave Mr. Douglas a half smile. "Yes," she said. "And we are finished with it now."

"We have quite a collection of animal specimens down in the basement," Mr. Douglas continued. "We'll have to show them in the library again soon. Haven't displayed them for some time." Mr. Douglas smiled. "Well, saunter along now. No galloping."

In the hallway outside the library, Jaime hung her head. "How could we be so wrong about everything? I was so sure I was right this time." She shook her head. "Next time, *please*, remind me about my active imagination before things get carried away."

Matt threw his hands in the air. "I did!" he said.

Outside the school, they watched as Mr. and Mrs. Rupert carried two large glass jars into the van.

"Do you need some help?" called Jaime.

Mrs. Rupert called back. "No thanks!" she

said. "This is the last load. We're just collecting up the old food jars left over from the cafeteria." She wiped her hands together. "They get pretty dusty, stored down in that basement." Mr. Rupert started up the van and waved.

"So that's what they're doing with the jars." Matt said as they sat down on the grass.

Then they watched as Mr. Turkle pulled his pickup truck into the parking lot. "We thought he was an alien!" Matt laughed out loud.

"Not just Mr. Turkle," Jaime began giggling. "We thought everybody was an alien." She rolled on the grass, grabbing her stomach and laughing uncontrollably. Matt laughed so hard that tears started to roll down his cheeks.

Finally, they stopped and sat up.

"That was pretty wild," said Matt as he wiped his face.

"That's for sure," agreed Jaime.

The last of the school buses pulled into the parking lot and the bell rang.

"Come on, we'd better not be late for class," Matt said, standing up and brushing himself off. As they walked across the grass, he asked, "Did you get your homework done?"

There was no answer. Matt turned around. Jaime had stopped a few steps back and was staring toward the roof of the school.

"Did you see that?" she asked. Her eyes were wide open. She covered her mouth and took a step back.

Matt glanced up. "See what?" he asked.

"There," said Jaime. She pointed at the roof.

"See that window? The one way up there?"

Matt looked. It was the window to the attic in the old part of the school. "I don't see anything," he said.

"I saw a ghost in that window! I saw a ghost in the attic of the school!" she said excitedly. "Come on!" she shouted, grabbing Matt's sleeve and pulling him toward the stairs.

"Here we go again," Matt sighed, rolling his eyes, as he followed Jaime toward their next adventure.

Suzan Reid has always loved writing. When she was little, she used to write stories for her dad (who was a janitor), and tuck them into his lunch bag so he wouldn't be lonely at work. Now she has written three picture books — *Grandpa Dan's Toboggan Ride*, *Follow That Bus!* and *The Meat Eaters Arrive*.

A full-time teacher, Suzan loves music, sports and swimming in her backyard pool. She lives in Westbank, British Columbia, with her husband, two daughters, cat and turtle.